This book belongs to

_____

King
Caspar's
Mines

Rushing River

Leopard's
Paradise

The City • The
Forest

The Eastern Frosting

...neyer Plains

...alley

R. Verbena

Toffee-Apple
Orchards

Look out for all the kingdom
of the Frosty Mountains books!

JESSICA JUNIPER
CRYSTAL COLDWATER
VALENTINA DE LA FROU

KINGDOM OF THE FROSTY MOUNTAINS

Laura-Bella

Emerald Everhart

Illustrated by
Patricia Ann Lewis-MacDougall

Modern Publishing
A Division of Unisystems, Inc.
New York, NY 10022
Printed in India
17895 – Feb 2009

MODERN
PUBLISHING
A DIVISION OF
UNISYSTEMS, INC.

Contents

Prologue

When I was a young ballerina, an admirer gave me a gift.

It was only a frosted-glass perfume bottle, filled with a sweet scent of lemon and orange. But my admirer told me that

the bottle was the most precious thing he could give, because there was a magical kingdom inside.

I didn't believe him at first.

But that night, I had a very special dream. I dreamed of a magical kingdom, the most beautiful land I'd ever seen, filled with delightful people and their very special animals. And the next time I danced, I thought of the kingdom, and suddenly I danced as I had never danced before. Every night that I wore the perfume, I danced

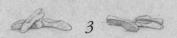

better than ever, until I was the most famous Ballerina in the world.

But one day, the old frosted-glass bottle was accidentally thrown away.

And from that day onward, I never danced so beautifully again.

I searched for the bottle high and low, but I never found it. I have since had many years to write down what I learned about the kingdom inside . . .

Within the bottle, behind the snow-capped Frosty Mountains, the kingdom is *divided into five parts. There are frozen Lakes in the north, warmer meadows in the southern Valley, stark gray Rocks in the west, and to the east, a deep, dark Forest.*

And the City. How could I forget the City? Silverberg, the capital, rising from the

Drosselmeyer Plains like a beautiful new jewel on an old ring.

From a distance, the houses seem to be piled on top of each other. Their brightly painted wooden roofs look as if they hold up the floors of the dwellings above as they wind around and around evermore narrow streets. And at the very top of the teetering pile is the biggest building of all: the Royal Palace. It is made from snow-white marble taken from the Frosty Mountains themselves, which glows in the

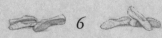

early morning sun and sparkles in the cold
night.

The Royal Palace is the home of the
King and Queen. But it is here, too, within

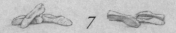

the marble walls of the palace, that you can find the kingdom's famous Royal Ballet School. This is where the most talented young ballerinas in the land become proper ballerinas-in-training, and really learn to dance. They travel from far and wide. Pale blonde Lake girls journey from the north, dark-haired Valley Dwellers come from the south. Gray-eyed ballerinas travel from the western Rocks, and green-eyed Forest girls make their way from the east. The City girls have no need to come quite so far.

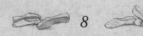

Of course, they all bring their pets. Each kingdom dweller has their own animal companion. And these animals can talk — talk just like you and me! Lake Dwellers keep Arctic foxes or snow leopards, while Valley Dwellers keep small tigers, monkeys, or exotic birds. Strong, sturdy Rock Dwellers enjoy the company of sheep, goats, and donkeys, while Forest Dwellers keep black bears and leopards. Every City Dweller keeps an eagle.

Out there, somewhere, is my old

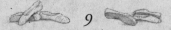

frosted-glass perfume bottle.

Out there, somewhere, are the ballerinas-in-training who inspired me — Jessica Juniper, Crystal Coldwater, Laura-Bella Bergamotta, Valentina de la Frou, and Ursula of the Boughs.

And they will wait for you, until the day that you find them.

Emerald Everhart

CHAPTER ONE
Bad News

In the kingdom of the Frosty Mountains, the Royal Ballet School was starting its spring term.

In Silverberg, the kingdom's capital city, the crocodils and the daffodaisies

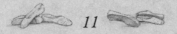

were in bloom and the trees were bursting into pink-and-white blossom. SpringSprung Day, the official start of spring, was just around the corner, and the whole kingdom was waiting to celebrate at the SpringSprung Festival.

Travelers would come to Silverberg from the northern Lake, the southern Valley, the eastern Forest and the western Rocks to join in the Festival. There would be street stalls, and entertainers, and a big Masked Ball for lots of

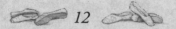

important grown-ups at the Royal Palace. Everyone was very excited.

But Jessica Juniper and her four best friends were even more excited than most. They would be performing a special dance for the SpringSprung Concert, at the start of the Masked Ball. They had all worked hard on their steps over the holiday, and now that the new term was starting, the concert was only a week away.

"Has anyone seen Laura-Bella?"

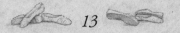

Jessica asked her friends Crys, Valentina, and Ursula, as they all unpacked their things in the Beginners' dormitory. "She must be so excited about SpringSprung."

Laura-Bella was a Valley Dweller, from the warm south of the kingdom. She had told her friends how much she longed for the warmer days of spring.

"No, but you know Laura-Bella's always late for everything," smiled Crys. "Unless Mr. Melchior gets his way."

Mr. Melchior was Laura-Bella's small and very bossy pet tiger. All the ballerinas-in-training kept special pets, who were rather scared of Mr. Melchior.

But suppertime came and went and

neither Laura-Bella nor Mr. Melchior were anywhere to be seen.

"Lost your little pal?" sneered Rubellina Goodfellow, the Chancellor's daughter, as she and her friend Jo-Jo passed by on the way out of the dining hall.

"None of your business, Rubellina," said Jessica.

"My daddy's the most important man in the kingdom," said Rubellina, "so *everything's* my business." She waved her hands in the air. "Don't you think my hands would look nice with beautiful silver rings?" she asked Jo-Jo. "And silver bangles on my wrists?"

And she and Jo-Jo, and their pet eagles, burst into giggles.

"What *is* she going on about? Silver rings and bangles?" Crys wondered in a low voice. "Do you think that's got something to do with Laura-Bella?"

"I don't know," said Jessica, stroking the soft, silky ears of her pet donkey, Sinbad. "But if Rubellina *does* know something, it can't be very good."

It was only as the girls were getting under their pink-and-gold quilts later that night that Laura-Bella and Mr. Melchior burst into the

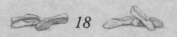

dormitory and hurried along to Laura-Bella's bed.

She threw herself on top of the quilt, and then burst into terrible sobs.

One look at Mr. Melchior's face told her friends that something was very wrong. The tiger was not looking as stern as usual. His face wore an expression of terrible worry.

"Laura-Bella, Mr. Melchior, what's happened?" asked Jessica, scrambling out of bed and running over.

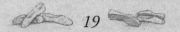

"It's awful." Laura-Bella lifted her head from the pillow. "We had the happiest holiday ever! We played in my family's orange orchard every morning, and picnicked by the waterfall every afternoon, and stayed out watching the stars in the lemon grove every night."

Her friends stared at each other. Sinbad the donkey spoke for them all. "What's so awful about that?"

This produced a fresh round of sobbing from Laura-Bella, so Mr.

Melchior took up the story.

"We're going to lose the farm."

Everybody gasped.

"Chancellor Godwin Goodfellow sent Laura-Bella's parents a letter," Mr. Melchior continued. His whiskers were trembling. "He owns the land their farm is on, and he's just discovered there is silver beneath the earth. Unless Laura-Bella's family can find the money to buy the land from the Chancellor by midnight on SpringSprung Day, he's going to throw them out!"

"He can't do that!" said Valentina.

"He can," sighed Mr. Melchior. "And he's going to do even worse. He's going to turn the farm into a huge silver mine."

Now Jessica understood why Rubellina Goodfellow had been giggling about silver jewelery. She had known her father was trying to take Laura-Bella's farm. "How much money does the Chancellor want?" she asked.

"One thousand marks!" sobbed Laura-Bella.

"*One thousand marks?*" This was more money than the girls had ever heard of.

"My mom and dad have begged and borrowed but they can only come up with 900 marks." Laura-Bella sat up and stared at her friends. Her eyes were red and swollen with days of crying, and her long dark hair was sticking out like a haystack. "There's no way of finding the last hundred marks. Mom and Dad are

packing up all our things, and I'll never go back to the farm again!"

Even 100 marks was a huge amount of money, but a plan was starting to form in Jessica's mind.

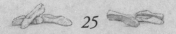

"Laura-Bella," she said, "maybe we can help you raise the rest of the money."

"By midnight on SpringSprung Day? But that's only a week away!" cried Valentina. Her eagle, Olympia, squawked in agreement.

"Besides, even Valentina only gets seven marks in pocket money each term," Crys said to Jessica. "How could we possibly scrape together a hundred marks?"

Now that Jessica had started, she could not stop. "We'll have to *earn* the money. Each of us is good at different things, aren't we? Well, we can use our talents to raise the cash! Crys, you could give extra ballet coaching to girls in our class, couldn't you?"

Crys nodded. "Happy to help."

"We'll do anything," added Pollux, her pet white fox, in his soft voice. He spoke so seldom that everyone stared at him.

"And Ursula," Jessica continued, "you've got such a lovely singing voice, you could sing in the Common Rooms in the evenings, and leave out a hat for coins."

Ursula, who was dreadfully shy, looked as though she would rather die than do any such thing, but her little

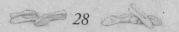

black bear, Dorothea, spoke up for her. "Of course she will."

"Oooh!" squealed Valentina. "And I could do makeovers! You know how good I am at hair and make-up."

"And I'll write stories, and sell them," said Jessica, who loved writing stories nearly as much as she loved dancing.

"*We'll* write stories, and sell them,"

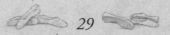

corrected Sinbad, who loved telling stories nearly as much as . . . well, Sinbad loved telling stories more than anything in the world.

Now Laura-Bella was drying her tears. "I've brought bags and bags of my father's lemons and oranges back to school with me," she said. "I make the best lemon-and-orangeade you've ever tasted."

"Then you can make lemon-and-orangeade, and sell lemon-and-orangeade!" Jessica said. "We'll raise the hundred marks in no time at all. Then we'll see the look on the Chancellor's face!"

"*And* on Rubellina's," said Sinbad happily.

CHAPTER TWO
The Lemon-and-Orangeade Stall

The next day, the girls could hardly wait to finish lessons so that they could spend more time on their tasks.

After supper, Jessica and Sinbad found a quiet corner and lots of paper,

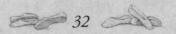

and began to write their stories. Crys spread the word that she was going to coach extra ballet, and took the names of everyone who wanted her help. Valentina put up a poster announcing that she would give makeovers for one mark per appointment, and decided that Ursula would be her first model.

"I'll give you a fantastic new look before you go and sing," Valentina told Ursula, taking her off to the dormitory.

Laura-Bella begged one of the palace

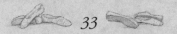

cooks to let her and Mr. Melchior make their lemon-and-orangeade in a corner of the kitchen.

"Do you really think this will work, Mr. Melchior?" Laura-Bella asked, as she absentmindedly weighed out huge bowls of sugar.

"Not if you put *that* much sugar in," said Mr. Melchior, who was peeling the fruit with his sharp claws. "Your customers' teeth will fall out."

"Not the drink, Mr. Melchior! Do

you think we'll raise the money in time to save our home?"

Mr. Melchior looked up at Laura-Bella's pleading eyes. The task seemed almost hopeless to him, but he knew he had to keep her spirits up. "With good hard work, almost anything is possible," he said.

It was not quite an answer to her question, but it brought a smile to her face.

Half an hour later, after every single juicy orange and sharp lemon had been squeezed till the last drop, mixed with the right amount of sugar and put to chill in the huge icebox, Laura-Bella and Mr. Melchior went to find a teacher to ask for special permission to go into the town.

The first teacher they saw was Master Lysander, whom they all secretly called Mustard Stockings, thanks to the horrible yellow stockings he always wore. He was the nastiest teacher in the school as well as being Chancellor Godwin Goodfellow's nephew, so there was no

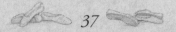

way Laura-Bella was going to ask *him*. He gave them both a suspicious look as they passed him by, but fortunately Mistress Hawthorne, the jolly Gym teacher, appeared in the corridor.

"You have to go into town to buy claw clippers?" echoed Mistress Hawthorne, at Laura-Bella's request.

"Yes, Mistress Hawthorne. Mr. Melchior's claws have gotten very long."

Mr. Melchior waved a paw at Mistress Hawthorne, splaying his claws.

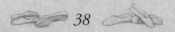

"It could be *terribly* dangerous," he said.

Mistress Hawthorne's pet goat let out a nervous bleat, and Mistress

Hawthorne herself took a large step backward.

"Here's your permission slip, dear," she said, scribbling hastily on her pad of paper.

"And why don't you buy that *dear, kind* tiger a big bag of sweets too," suggested her goat. "We really don't want him getting hungry!"

The evening was still light as Laura-Bella and Mr. Melchior hurried down into Silverberg with their jugs of lemon-

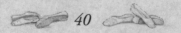

and-orangeade, and there was the sweet smell of daffodaisies in the air. They found a bench under a pretty berry blossom tree in the marketplace, and soon a line had formed. The City Dwellers were full of mounting SpringSprung excitement, and a cold glass of lemon-and-orangeade under the berry blossom seemed the perfect way to spend this beautiful spring evening.

"One mark a cup!" Mr. Melchior

sang out, as Laura-Bella served the drinks and took the money. "Only one mark!"

But Laura-Bella was quickly beginning to think that they ought to have asked for two marks a cup. The lemon-and-orangeade was so popular that they were close to running out after only half the line had been served. Disappointed, she jingled the twenty marks in her pocket as she poured the very last glass for a beaming lady at the head of the line.

"This is the best lemon-and-orangeade I've ever tasted!" said the beaming lady. "You here from the Valley for SpringSprung?"

"Yes," lied Laura-Bella, not wanting her drinks stall to be reported back to school.

"Well, Silverberg's the best place for SpringSprung," said the lady. "A big fair here in the marketplace, and a posh Masked Ball up at the palace. The ballerinas-in-training give a special

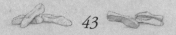

43

concert, you know."

"Oh, really?" mumbled Laura-Bella.

"Course, that's not for the likes of us. Only the upper crust ever get to see the ballerinas dance. The lords and ladies, and that pompous old twerp Chancellor Goodfellow."

Laura-Bella could think of even more names to call him.

"It's unfair, I always think," the lady continued, turning to leave. "Ordinary City Dwellers would pay good money to

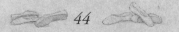

see our famous ballerinas, but we never have the chance."

Laura-Bella watched the lady walk away. An idea was forming in her mind.

"We've made . . . twenty-one marks in total," Mr. Melchior said in surprise. "Not bad for a night's work. If the others have made the same amount each, we'll have our hundred marks already. Let's hurry back to the palace and find out."

CHAPTER THREE
A New Plan

When they arrived back at school, Laura-Bella and Mr. Melchior soon knew the news was not good. The Beginners' dormitory was nearly empty, apart from Rubellina and Jo-Jo giggling

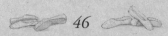

nastily at one end, and Laura-Bella's friends in a terrible commotion at the other.

"You've missed all the fun," snickered Rubellina. Laura-Bella ignored her, and hurried by.

Sinbad and Jessica were arguing. Valentina and Olympia were sulking. Crys was pacing the floor, with Pollux wrapped around her shoulders. And Ursula was lying on her bed, her head buried beneath her small bear, Dorothea.

"I told you one *mark* per story, not one *penny*!" Jessica shouted at Sinbad. "You let everyone buy a story for one-tenth of the right price!"

"If you'd let me write the stories instead of you, we *could* have charged one mark!" Sinbad shouted back. "Nobody was going to pay one whole mark for your silly stories about bunny rabbits and gnomes."

"Nobody was going to pay *anything* for your stories about ghosts and goblins and cut-throat pirates," said Jessica. "You'd have frightened the life out of everyone."

"I still don't see why I had to give back *all* the money I made from my makeovers," Valentina was pouting. "It was only Carolina Kirshbaum whose hair turned green."

"And Nettie Treehouse whose hair turned purple," said Crys.

"Huh!" said Valentina.

"Bah!" squawked Olympia.

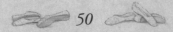

"And Jemima Nightfrost whose lips puffed up like a fish," Crys continued. "And Linda Stone whose eyelashes dropped out. And Maria Monticello who –"

"All right!" yelled Valentina. "It's not like your ballet lessons were any more of a success!"

"They might have been," Crys stopped pacing, "if you hadn't made all my pupils' hair turn funny colors so they spent the evening crying in the bathroom."

"Oh dear," said Laura-Bella, sitting down on the bed beside Ursula. "Please tell me your singing made some money, at least."

"She never managed to sing after all," said Jessica.

"Why not?" asked Laura-Bella.

Ursula lifted her head from underneath Dorothea's fur. Her hair was a nasty shade of blue and her eyebrows a rather disturbing egg-yolk yellow.

"Valentina gave me a makeover

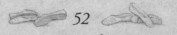

first," Ursula said miserably.

Laura-Bella would have laughed if she hadn't felt so desperate. "So how much money have you made altogether?" she asked her friends.

After a very rapid count, the final total, including Laura-Bella's twenty-one marks, was twenty-three marks and four pence.

"Then there's only one thing to do," said Laura-Bella, gathering the others around her bed so that Rubellina could not hear a thing. "A lady in town told me that the City Dwellers never get to see us ballerinas dance, and they'd pay good money to do so."

"But we aren't allowed to perform without permission. And we can't dance anywhere but here at the palace," said Valentina.

Jessica was thinking hard. "And how would we sneak out of the palace? We'd never all get permission slips at the same time."

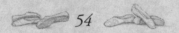

Laura-Bella took a deep breath. "We could go on SpringSprung night, after we've done the concert here. The guards will all have drunk far too much SpringSprung punch to even notice we're sneaking by, and all the teachers will be at the Masked Ball. Nobody would miss us for an hour or so."

"But if we got caught," said Sinbad, in far too loud a voice, "wouldn't we be executed or something?"

"No, Sinbad!" hissed Jessica. "We'd

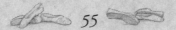

55

just be in big trouble."

"*Really* big trouble," said Laura-Bella. "We'd probably get expelled. So I don't blame any of you for refusing to join us."

"*Us?*" sighed Mr. Melchior. "I suppose that means it's already too late for me to refuse." But he gave Laura-Bella a gentle pat on the arm with his long tail.

"We'll do it, won't we, Sinbad?" said Jessica, popping a handful of lemon

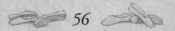

fizzicles into the donkey's mouth before he could disagree.

Crys and Pollux both nodded that they would join in.

"We really need you too, Ursula," said Laura-Bella. "You'll have to sing while we dance, as we won't have any music."

"But I've got blue hair!" cried Ursula.

"Oh, we'll fix that before SpringSprung Day," said Valentina. "And count me and Olympia in, too."

Laura-Bella's face lit up in the brightest smile they'd ever seen. "Thanks, everyone. You're the best friends in the whole kingdom. Now all we need is a plan."

CHAPTER FOUR
SpringSprung Night

Every day from then until SpringSprung Day itself, the ballerinas and their pets met in a huddle to go over the plan time and time again.

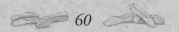

"Now, the marketplace will be the best place for us to dance," said Laura-Bella. "Olympia, once we've started, you must fly about the town to spread the word that the ballerinas-in-training are performing."

The eagle quivered with excitement.

"Pollux and Dorothea, you'll each have to take a hat around the crowd to collect the seventy-six marks and sixpence."

The quiet white fox and the little

bear both nodded.

"Sinbad, you've got to keep a look-out for anyone who might report us."

Sinbad thought about this. "Is that the *most* important job?"

"Oh, yes," everyone agreed. "By far the most important."

Sinbad waggled his long ears in delight. "Then I think I'll need a new hat."

Laura-Bella carried on. "And Mr. Melchior, the very moment we've got the

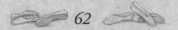

amount we need, you have to race all the way back to Mom and Dad in the Valley and give them every penny, before midnight passes."

Mr. Melchior stretched out his fast, powerful legs. "I will run like the wind,"

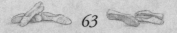

he said.

"And all *we* have to do," Laura-Bella told the other girls, "is practice and practice and practice our dance. The better we perform, the more money we'll make."

Coached by Crys in every spare moment they had, the girls were soon dancing better than ever. They prepared their sprite costumes and shoes more carefully than every other girl in the Beginners' class, knowing that they would have to last two performances on the same night. Valentina helped Ursula wash her hair and her eyebrows three times a day, until the last tinges of blue and yellow had faded.

Finally, SpringSprung Day itself dawned. Although the entire school was in a state of grand excitement about the SpringSprung Concert that evening, Laura-Bella and her friends were more nervous about their plans for after the concert.

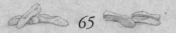 65

"That little gang seems very calm," Mustard Stockings said to Mistress Camomile suspiciously, as the two ballet teachers led them through a warm-up before the concert.

"Oh, we're not calm, not calm at all!" said Sinbad, clattering his hoofs about noisily and taking far too many deep breaths. "Never been *less* calm, in fact!"

"We're just really excited about SpringSprung," said Jessica hastily, trying to change the subject. "What a very lovely outfit, Mistress Camomile."

"It's for the Masked Ball," smiled Mistress Camomile, popping a pretty little cat mask over her eyes. "But you'll be all tucked up in bed by then, girls!"

The five exchanged glances, but said nothing.

It seemed like the concert was over in a flash. The audience of lords, ladies and courtiers cheered the Beginners' SpringSprite dance. Even the King and his pudgy eagle, sitting in the royal box, stayed awake for most of it. Chancellor Goodfellow, sitting beside the King, smiled far more than usual, clapping loudly when Rubellina had a few solo steps.

"He looks so pleased," Laura-Bella hissed to Jessica, as they passed each other during the polka. "Let's see his face when he finds out my parents can stop him from taking our farm after all."

Jessica only hoped Laura-Bella was right.

The girls hid in a corner backstage until all the other ballerinas-in-training had changed out of their costumes and been shooed away to bed. Then, as quietly as they could, they made their way down the dark corridors, past the dozing guards, and out of the palace.

The noise from the town center grew louder the closer they got, but the girls were still amazed to see the crowds and the sights when they reached the marketplace. Hundreds of City Dwellers,

dressed in their finest, bright silk cloaks
and hats, strolled about the square. There
were food and drink stalls, and fire-

jugglers, and a marching band, and a
puppet show. Sinbad sniffed longingly
in the direction of a stall selling

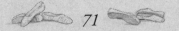

SpringSprung pudding, and was glad when the girls decided to perform their dance right beside it.

"Good luck, everyone," said Laura-Bella, as they took up their positions for the start of the SpringSprite dance. "The better we dance, the faster Mr. Melchior can take the money to my mom and dad!"

At Laura-Bella's signal, Ursula began to sing, and the dance began with Crys' solo.

"Quick, Olympia!" hissed Valentina, letting her eagle fly. "Go and spread the word."

But it looked as if they would hardly need Olympia's help after all. Amazed to see the ballerinas dancing in the marketplace, the crowds gathered so quickly that there was scarcely room for Pollux and Dorothea to make their way among them with their hats.

"That girl's a genius!" came cries from the crowd as Crys finished her solo, followed by *oooohs* and *aaaahs* as the other three joined in for the elegant polka.

Sinbad could hardly tear his eyes off the nearby SpringSprung puddings, steaming in their little checked cloths. His mouth was watering so much, it was all he could do to keep his eyes on the crowd. He tore himself away from the delicious stall and trotted off to keep watch by the entrance to the marketplace.

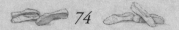

Suddenly, a little pudding was wafted under his nose. "Here, my fine Mr. Donkey, how would you like a tasty SpringSprung pudding?"

It was a tall man, in a fancy mask and

a long cloak.

"Wow!" said Sinbad. 'Are you sure?'

"It's all yours." The masked man watched as Sinbad bit into the warm, curranty dough. "What's going on over there? That's a huge crowd."

"The ballerinas-in-training are performing their SpringSprite dance," said Sinbad, through a mouthful of currants.

The man's eyes grew wide behind his

mask. "I see. Why, may I ask?"

"Oh, our friend Laura-Bella's got to raise the money to stop stinky, old Chancellor Goodfellow from stealing her farm."

"I *see*," said the masked man again. "And then what?"

"Well, then her pet tiger's going to race off to the Valley to give her mom and dad the money, just as soon as they've got enough." Sinbad polished off the last of his pudding. "Looking at the crowd, I should think that'll be quite soon. Now, you don't have any more of these puddings, do you?"

But the masked man had turned and was running away, back toward the palace.

It was only then that Sinbad noticed the mustard-colored stockings beneath his long black cloak.

CHAPTER FIVE
Tiger, Tiger

Sinbad raced as fast as he could to where Dorothea was handing her coin-filled hat over to Mr. Melchior.

"How much money do we have?" the donkey cried.

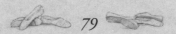

"The exact amount. Seventy-six marks and sixpence," said Mr. Melchior. "So now we have one hundred altogether."

"Then go!" Sinbad brayed. "We've been caught!"

"Caught?"

"Discovered!" Sinbad's ears were waving about. "I didn't know it was Mustard Stockings . . . I just thought he was a nice kind man giving me pudding . . . but now he knows everything!"

"You foolish, foolish donkey!" snapped Mr. Melchior, running along with Sinbad to warn the ballerinas.

Laura-Bella turned pale as she saw the two pets race through the crowd, and signaled to the others to stop dancing and follow her. A groan went through the crowd as the dance came to a hasty end.

"I must go at once," Mr. Melchior told Laura-Bella. "Mustard Stockings knows all about our plan."

"It's all my fault!" howled Sinbad.

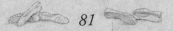

"It will be all right," said Jessica, helping Laura-Bella attach the special money belt around Mr. Melchior's middle. "The money's ready to go. Now we must try to get back to the palace before Mustard Stockings reports us."

"Run as fast as you can, Mr. Melchior! You must get there before midnight," called Laura-Bella, as the sleek little tiger sped off through the night.

With shaking legs and butterflies in their tummies, the five ballerinas-in-

training hurried back up the hill to the palace. The guards were still dozing in the corridors, which was a surprise.

"But the teachers are bound to be looking for us," whispered Valentina fearfully, as they tiptoed their way past the Great Hall.

But to their amazement, there was no angry commotion in the Great Hall. The Masked Ball was in full swing, and their teachers could be seen mixing with all the important guests. Mistress

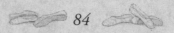

Hawthorne, whose mask could not disguise her plump cheeks, was dancing a tango with her goat, while Master Silas, the stern History of Ballet teacher, played peacemaker for Mistress Camomile and Master Jacques over a SpringSprung pudding.

Nobody seemed to know that the girls had sneaked out at all.

They hurried up the stairs to the dormitory, still sure there would be an angry teacher waiting. But the dormitory was dark and still, all the Beginners sleeping after their exciting evening dancing at the concert. Even Rubellina was asleep in her bed.

"We've got away with it," whispered Crys.

"But Mustard Stockings will never keep it a secret!" Jessica said.

"If we get into bed like we never went out, it'll be his word against ours," said Crys, pulling her quilt up over herself and Pollux.

Their hearts beating very fast, the others did the same.

"I'm sorry," said Sinbad in a very small voice. "I really didn't mean to get

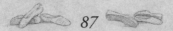

us into trouble."

"Don't worry about anything, Sinbad," Laura-Bella whispered back. "I don't think we're in trouble at all."

Knowing that the money was on its way to her parents' farm, Laura-Bella slept more soundly than she had in a week. She dreamt about Mr. Melchior's journey, racing southward toward the Valley with the sweet smell of the green meadows and the fruit orchards. He would sleep the night there, beneath the

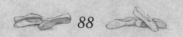

stars, and when the dawn came, he would awaken with warm sunlight on his striped fur, to a Valley breakfast of –

"Laura-Bella! Wake up!"

Laura-Bella opened her eyes. It was definitely dawn, but the pale-blue dawn of the City, not the golden glow of the Valley. And Mr. Melchior was standing beside her, but he was not sleek and triumphant from his race.

He was breathless and ragged, and his paws were bleeding dreadfully.

"Mr. Melchior!" she gasped.

As she washed the blood away in the bathroom, Mr. Melchior told her what had happened.

"There was a trap," he managed to say. "A trap was set on the road to the Valley. It caught my front paws so that I couldn't move. Then three men appeared from nowhere. They had the hoods of their cloaks up, but one of them was Mustard Stockings all right. I'd know those yellow legs anywhere!"

"Your poor paws!" sobbed Laura-Bella.

Mr. Melchior's head drooped. "It's much worse than that. They took my money belt. Everything's gone, Laura-Bella. Every single penny. And now midnight has passed, and your parents never got the money, and the farm is gone after all."

CHAPTER SIX
Royal Appointment

Laura-Bella awakened her friends, and held a hushed meeting in the bathroom.

"So that's why Mustard Stockings didn't report us! He must have gone straight to Chancellor Goodfellow and

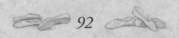

told him about our plan to buy the farm," said Jessica, while Sinbad stroked Mr. Melchior's sore paws with the tips of his ears, and wailed.

"So we didn't get expelled, but the money's gone," said Crys.

"Not if I have anything to do with it," said Laura-Bella. Her cheeks were very pink. "Nobody messes with my tiger and gets away with it. I don't care how much trouble I'm in – I'm going to go to Mistress Odette, and tell her

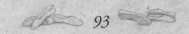

everything!" She squeezed her friends' hands. "Now, don't worry. I won't get you four into trouble as well. I'll say it was only me who did the dancing in the marketplace."

"Don't be silly," said Ursula,

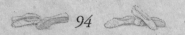

speaking up for them all. "We're all in this together."

So, with butterflies in their tummies more than ever before, the five friends and their pets made their way through the silent corridors to the headmistress' rooms. After a few sharp knocks on the door, Mistress Odette pulled it open. She was wearing a peach-colored dressing gown and a very surprised expression.

"Ballerinas! What's happening? Is

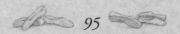

there an emergency?"

"Yes, there is," declared Laura-Bella. "Chancellor Goodfellow has stolen our farm, and our money, and we danced in the marketplace but we're very sorry, and Mr. Melchior has bleeding paws, and you have to tell the King so that Chancellor Goodfellow can be stopped before he turns everything into silver!"

Then she and Sinbad both burst into tears.

Mistress Odette gathered them all

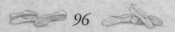

into her sitting room. She found bandages for Mr. Melchior, mugs of hot white chocolate for the girls, and an enormous handkerchief for Sinbad, who looked as though he would rather have had the hot chocolate.

"Now," she said. "Tell me everything."

As Laura-Bella and the others told the whole story, Mistress Odette's face grew more and more shocked, particularly when they told her about their secret performance in the

98

marketplace. But she listened all the way through, and made some notes in a notepad when they told her about the stolen money. Then she inspected Mr. Melchior's paws, and questioned him about the hooded men. She gave him a little pat behind the ears when he had finished, but when she turned back to face the ballerinas, her face was like thunder.

"Go back to your dormitory," she said, "and wait there until you hear from me again."

"But Mistress Odette, the King must be told –"

Mistress Odette silenced Laura-Bella with one look. "You are in quite enough trouble already," she said quietly, "so please do what I say."

They trooped back into the dormitory just as all the other Beginners were starting to get out of bed.

Everybody stared at the girls' sullen faces and red eyes. "What's happened?"

some of the Beginners asked. "What's going on?"

Rubellina could not hide her smiles. "SpringSprung has come and gone!" she sang as she dressed for breakfast. "I think *poor* Laura-Bella is going to have to move . . .."

She was only silenced by a low growl from Mr. Melchior.

The dormitory fell very silent after everybody else had gone off to breakfast.

"I'm very sorry," Laura-Bella finally said in a small voice. "We're all going to be expelled, and it's my fault."

"It's all right," said Jessica, trying to keep everyone's spirits up. "Look on the bright side – at least we're missing morning lessons! Don't forget there's a History of Ballet test this morning."

But as the hours went by, they started to long for morning lessons, History of Ballet tests and all.

"They're probably summoning our

parents," Valentina began, as the palace bell rang eleven. "They'll come and tell us to pack . . . ."

Just then, the door opened.

It was not their parents, but Mistress Odette. And walking behind her were the Seventeen Royal Flugelhorn Players.

This could only mean one thing.

"Stand up, girls," said Mistress Odette. "The King is coming."

Everybody scrambled to their feet as King Caspar came into the dormitory. To

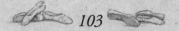

their amazement, he was followed by Mustard Stockings and Chancellor Goodfellow. The Chancellor was wearing

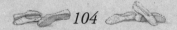

his usual black robes, and he was not smiling.

"Not looking too happy, Chancellor," Laura-Bella murmured to herself.

"Your Majesty, please meet Laura-Bella Bergamotta and her friends," said Mistress Odette, giving the ballerinas-in-training an icy stare. "These are the girls I was telling you about."

"*Were* you?" said the King, whose memory was as short as his eagle was pudgy.

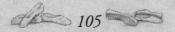

"Yes, Your Majesty," said Mistress Odette, with great patience. "Laura-Bella is the girl whose farm was *stolen*," she cast her icy stare over at Chancellor Goodfellow, "along with 100 marks."

"Ah," said the King, remembering. "A bad business, very bad."

Now Chancellor Goodfellow stepped forward. "But, as I'm sure you also remember, Your Majesty, these girls have broken school rules, and —"

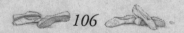

"That's enough out of you, Godwin!" snapped Mistress Odette, silencing the Chancellor as though he were a naughty pupil. "Your Majesty, you may continue."

"I'm sure I *may*," said the King, stroking his eagle, "but I'm not altogether sure I *can*. I can't for the life of me remember who this Bella-Burger girl is! My apologies, dear," he added, turning to Laura-Bella.

Mistress Odette disguised a sigh.

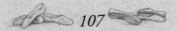

"What I think you were going to say,
Your Majesty, is that Laura-Bella's home
is safe."

Laura-Bella clutched her headboard. "I . . . beg your pardon . . . ."

"Chancellor Goodfellow has agreed to sell the farm to your parents for 900 marks," Mistress Odette continued. "I believe they have already paid him that sum of money. Isn't that correct, Chancellor?"

The Chancellor bowed his head. "Yes," he said, through teeth so clenched the girls could hardly hear him.

"And he has agreed to give that

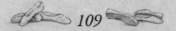

hundred marks he *happens* to have in that money bag to the poor children of the town." Mistress Odette's voice was firm. "Isn't *that* correct, Chancellor?"

The Chancellor could not even reply now, but he waved the money bag in agreement.

"And he and Master Lysander have agreed to apologize to you, Laura-Bella, and to you, Mr. Melchior, for the *very silly and nasty joke* they played on you," finished Mistress

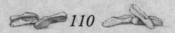

Odette seriously.

"It wasn't a joke," said Sinbad under his breath.

"I think Mistress Odette knows that," Jessica whispered back.

The Chancellor and Mustard Stockings bowed very low before Laura-Bella and Mr. Melchior, muttering "Our apologies" in furious voices.

"Then that's that!" said Mistress Odette. "Now I simply require a private word with my pupils."

"Delightful to meet you all," said the King, as the Chancellor and Mustard Stockings escorted him outside. "I'll

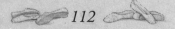

remember this forever!"

"He won't," said Mistress Odette, as the dormitory door closed behind them, "but you five *will* remember this: You will never, never break a school rule like that again."

"Yes, Mistress Odette," they all said, waiting for the announcement that they were to be expelled.

"But you are good friends to each other, and that is a very important thing." The headmistress suddenly smiled. "Apart

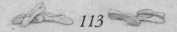

from your rule-breaking, you are exactly the kind of pupils that this ballet school needs."

Laura-Bella let out a whoop of delight, and flung her arms around her friends. "So we've saved the farm, and we're not expelled after all?"

"Quite right," said Mistress Odette. "And I do believe that if you hurry, you will just be in time for your History of Ballet test."

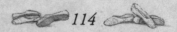

THE END

Manners

Our Home is Your Home

The kingdom's inhabitants are warm and welcoming. Every house in the kingdom has a front doormat that reads "Our Home Is Your Home," and your hosts will do everything they can to make you feel comfortable. But do not take this too far. If you are a couch potato in your own

home, fond of dropping candy wrappers on the floor and putting your feet up on the best furniture, do not do this in somebody else's house. (Donkeys are particularly known for these bad habits. They simply do not seem to care where they put their great big hoofs.) Instead, arrive on time, neatly dressed, and bring a little gift to show your thanks. A beautiful posy of daffodaisies is always delightful; a bunch of crocodils is usually not.

For What You are
About to Receive

When sitting down to a meal, every good kingdom host will insist that you take the biggest portion of the food they have cooked. This may be a sweet, sticky toffee apple torte, or a delicious selection of freshly made ice buns. On the other hand, it may be a sardine stew or (if you are very unlucky) a Sunday slop-pot. No matter what you are served, eat with gusto, and always ask for seconds. Asking for thirds is very bad manners indeed. Are you paying attention, Sinbad?

A Menu of Rules

Kingdom dwellers will be extremely impressed if you understand their many different eating customs, so why not try out one or two? For example, snowpea soup is always eaten with a special snowpea soup-spoon, unless it is the third Thursday of the month, when it is sipped through a snowpea sip-straw, or the second Wednesday of the month, when it is eaten from a snowpea sup-cup. You see? Easy! Or why not show off how much you know about white chocolate tarts? The tart must only be served on a marble platter, and the first slice must be cut by the youngest member of the household, unless it is raining outside, in which case the first slice must be cut by the oldest member of the household. And if it is sunny, or snowing, or if there are more than three clouds in the sky, then no white chocolate tarts can be served at all.

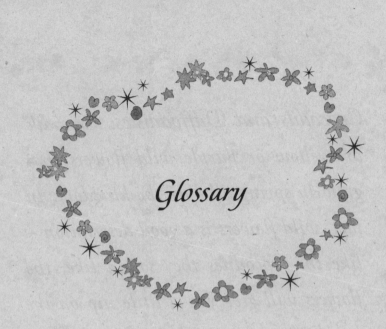

Glossary

Cinnamon Twists: *Long, thin doughnuts that are twisted into a double knot before being freshly fried and then sprinkled with cinnamon sugar. A speciality of Silverberg. Donkeys love them.*

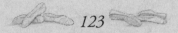

Crocodils and Daffodaisies: Crocodils are yellow or purple wild flowers that grow in spring all over the kingdom. In fact, wild flowers is a good description — like the crocodiles they sound like, the flowers will give you a little nip on the hand if you try to pick them before they are ready. Daffodaisies are less dangerous. They are tall white-and-yellow daisies the size of daffodils, and perfect for making into long daffodaisy chains.

Frosting Stones: Precious stones mined from the Frosty Mountains themselves. They come in several colors — red, green, blue, and a deep amber — but the most prized of all are the colorless stones, more beautiful even than our own diamonds. The stones come out of the mountain just as they are, with no need for cutting or polishing. Finding a particularly large Frosting Stone could make you wealthy, but mining them is dangerous and difficult work.

Hot Buttered Flumpets: These are a little bit like the crumpets you eat for tea, but they taste softer and slightly sweeter, and they are shaped like fingers. They are always served piping hot, with melted butter oozing through the holes.

Ice Buns: Made for special occasions in the Lakes, these buns look plain on the outside but are filled with creamy pink-and-white ice cream on the inside. Be careful when you bite in!

Iced White Chocolate Drops: An expensive treat that only the very rich can afford. These chocolate drops are found by divers inside seashells at the very bottom of the northern Lake. They stay ice-cold right up until they are popped into your mouth, where they slowly melt.

Icicle Bicycles: Quite simply, bicycles carved from blocks of ice. They are the best way to travel from one side of the frozen

Lake to the other, as the icy wheels speed you across without any danger of skidding or slipping. But be warned, and pack a cushion — or the icy seat will leave your bottom extremely cold.

Lemon Fizzicles: Lemon-flavored chewy sweets that fizz with tiny bubbles inside your mouth.

Raspberry Flancakes: Flancakes are yeasty, flaky pancakes that rise up to two or four inches thick when you cook them in a special flancake pan. Their outside is brown and rich with butter, their inside light and airy. Flancakes can be made in any flavor, but raspberry is the most popular. Donkeys love them, too.

Scoffins: Halfway between a scone and a muffin. They are best served fresh from the oven, split in two, and spread with snowberry jam.

Snowberries: Round, plump, juicy berries that grow all over the kingdom throughout the winter. The snowberries from the south and the west are very dark pink, while the ones that grow in the east and the north are red in color. Snowberries are always eaten cooked — in jams, flancakes, waffles or muffins — where they taste sweet but tart at the same time. Don't make the mistake of eating one straight from the garden, however tasty it looks. Uncooked snowberries are delicious, but they pop open in your mouth and fill it with a juice so sticky that your teeth are instantly glued together. This can take a whole morning to wear off.

SpringSprung Day: The official first day of spring, and a big day for the inhabitants of the kingdom after a long, cold winter. SpringSprung Day is marked with a big festival in Silverberg, but the Valley Dwellers throw parties in their own homes for those who would rather not travel the long distance to the City. For many, the highlight of the festivities is the SpringSprung pudding (see below), though many delicious delicacies are served, including lemon-and-orangeade.

SpringSprung Pudding: A sponge pudding, filled with plump currants and chewy, dried snowberries, this is steamed in a huge pudding basin and served in thick slices, sprinkled with sugar, on

SpringSprung Day. One pudding will normally feed ten hungry people. Sinbad can eat a whole pudding all by himself, with room for more.

Toffee Apple Torte: The speciality of the Grand Café and Tea-Rooms in Silverberg. This tart is made with delicate slices of the fruits that grow in the toffee-apple orchards in the deep south of the Valley, then served warm with toffee-butter sauce.

Who's Who in the kingdom of the Frosty Mountains

The girls and their pets

Jessica Juniper – *Ballerina from the western Rocks*

Sinbad – *Jessica's pet donkey*

Crystal Coldwater – *Ballerina from the northern Lake*

Pollux – *Crystal's pet white fox*

Laura-Bella Bergamotta – *Ballerina from the southern Valley*

Mr. Melchior – *Laura-Bella's pet tiger*

Ursula of the Boughs – *Ballerina from the eastern Forest*

Dorothea – *Ursula's pet bear*

Valentina de la Frou – *Ballerina from the City*

Olympia – *Valentina's pet eagle*

Some other ballerinas

Rubellina Goodfellow – *Ballerina from the City, and the Chancellor's daughter*

Jo-Jo Marshall – *Another ballerina from the City, and Rubellina's best friend*

The Teachers

Mistress Odette – *the Headmistress*

Mistress Camomile – *a Ballet teacher*

Master Lysander – *another Ballet teacher, also known as Mustard Stockings*

Master Silas – *the History of Ballet teacher*

Mistress Hawthorne – *the Gym teacher*

Mistress Babette – *the Costume, Hair, and Makeup teacher*

Master Jacques – *the Mime teacher*

The Royal Party

King Caspar – *the King*

Queen Mab – *the Queen*

Chancellor Godwin Goodfellow – *the kingdom's Chancellor*

Don't miss the first book in the series

Jessica Juniper

It's Jessica's first day at ballet school
and she wants to make a good
impression. So when the teachers think
she has played a practical joke on the
Chancellor's daughter, Jessica and Sinbad
the donkey have to try extra hard. But
things keep going wrong.
Can Jessica prove her innocence?

**Twinkle your toes with the ballerinas
and their talking pets!**

KINGDOM OF THE
FROSTY MOUNTAINS

Jessica Juniper

by
Emerald
Everhart

Inside the perfume bottle
a magical kingdom is waiting for you . . .

Don't miss the second book in the series

Crystal Coldwater

The ballerinas-in-training are excited –
they have to write about their favorite
ballerina, Eva Snowdrop. So why is Crys
so upset? Even her fox, Pollux, can't
soothe her. Can the girls find out? And
how will icicle bicycles help?

**Twinkle your toes with the ballerinas
and their talking pets!**

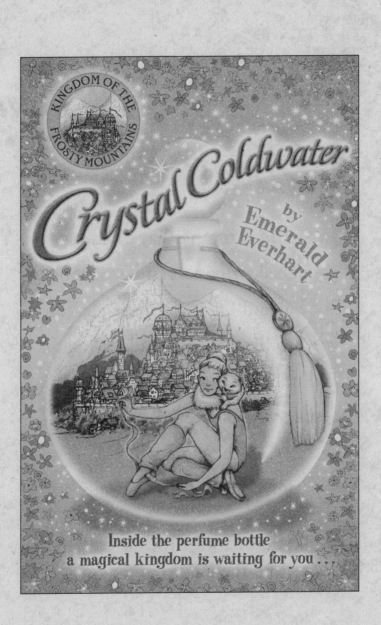

KINGDOM OF THE FROSTY MOUNTAINS

Crystal Coldwater

by Emerald Everhart

Inside the perfume bottle
a magical kingdom is waiting for you...

Don't miss the fourth book in the series

Valentina de la Frou

Valentina's mother has decided to
send Valentina to another school.
But Val and Olympia the eagle don't
want to leave their friends. Olympia
would miss her hero, Sinbad the donkey,
desperately. Besides, they love ballet!
Can the girls help Val
prove she deserves to stay?

**Twinkle your toes with the ballerinas
and their talking pets!**

KINGDOM OF THE FROSTY MOUNTAINS

Valentina de la Frou

by
Emerald
Everhart

Inside the perfume bottle
a magical kingdom is waiting for you . . .